Monica the Monkey Grasshopper

The brightly colored monkey grasshopper is one of the world's most beautiful insects. With few visible flowering plants in tropical rainforests, insects have been referred to as the "flowers of the jungle". This species of grasshopper has ears on the sides of its abdomen.

Grayson the Grasshopper Sparrow

Grasshopper sparrows are named for one of their calls—a quiet buzz that sounds much like a grasshopper. Male sparrows sing only a few months of the year during the nesting season. Intricately patterned in brown, white, and black, these birds are well camouflaged with the remote grasslands in Florida's interior where they live.

Spike the Sparrow Hawk

The sparrowhawk is small-bodied with relatively short, rounded wings, long legs, and a strongly hooked beak. The male is dark grey above, while the underparts are pale and distinctively marked with fine reddish-brown barring. They have a pale line above the eye and a white patch on the chin.

Hugo the Hawksbill Turtle of the Sea

The majority of hawksbill sea turtles live in tropical regions of both the Atlantic and Pacific Oceans. They love rocky areas and stay mainly in shallow waters. It is unusual to find them more than 65 feet below the surface. They are good climbers on sandy areas where they deposit their eggs.

MOLLY the MANATEE

CHIC CARIAGA

FOR KAY for her
inspiration, for her dedication, for
putting up with me as my high school
English teacher; this book is proudly
dedicated to Kay Tawney. Teachers matter
more than we want to admit. Thank you.
And FOR LAURIE Steinemer: it has
been a long road since we first discussed
"The Vanity of the Manatee" over dinner
one cold winter's night in 2013. The
journey is complete. Thank
you for your inspiration.
FROM CHIC

FOR JACOB for
believing in me before
I believed in myself and
for all the crazy projects,
some that may have
only mattered to us.
FROM LIZA

FOR MY PARENTS
dedicated with love to my
parents, Lash, and Cyrette
Sanford who made my
childhood magical,
adventuresome,
and fun.
FROM CECE

AN ADVENTURE IN SELF-DISCOVERY

a manatee leaves her pod in search of
something different and meets many
colorful animal friends along the way

COOL WATER RIPPLE BOOKS
© 2016 by Chic Cariaga (copyright pending)
edited by CeCe Curran & illustrated by Liza Donovan
All rights reserved.

For more information contact:
Chic Cariaga
PO Box 489
Lockhart, SC 29364
chiccariaga@ aol.com

Library of Congress Cataloging-in-Publication Data
ISBN: 978-0-9974705-0-5
printed in Korea

Molly the Manatee

CHIC CARIAGA

cool
water
ripple books
CHARLOTTE NORTH CAROLINA

A solitary figure could be seen swimming outside a group of manatees called a pod. MOLLY THE MANATEE was shy and felt as though she did not fit in with the other manatees. Molly was smart and was a very sweet manatee. She simply wanted to be something other than what she was. Molly separated further away from her pod and began swimming down the Manatee River on her adventure to become something else. And thus begins the tale of a manatee—Molly's quest of discovery.

Molly first came across a creature drinking from the river.

"Excuse me, my name is Molly. Who are you?"

"I am **WILLIAM THE WOLF**, the leader of my pack."

Molly stated, "I want to be a leader. Can I be a wolf?"

William the Wolf replied, "Of course not, look at my teeth. You do not have the right kind of teeth to be a wolf."

Molly looked sad.

William, feeling sorry for Molly said, "Perhaps you could be a wolf spider."

William pointed in the direction of an old tree.

"Wilson the Wolf Spider lives in a hole over there", William said as he turned and snuck into the woods.

Molly swiftly swam over to the tree and shouted, "Hello!"

An old spider crawled out of his hole. "Who is out here yelling at my door?"

The spider had many eyes and wore funny looking glasses.

"Are you WILSON THE WOLF SPIDER?"

"Of course I am. Why do you ask?"

"Because I want to be a wolf spider too."

"Ha, you do not have enough eyes to be a wolf spider". The spider looked

sadly at Molly as she seemed upset by his rejection.

"But, I bet you can be a spider monkey", Wilson said as he pointed at the

tree above. And with that, Wilson slipped back into his dwelling.

Excitement came to Molly's eyes when she saw movement in the tree.

A monkey was swinging by his tail and throwing pecan shells at floating leaves.

Molly cried out, "Excuse me sir, what is your name?"

The monkey swung from branch to branch until he finally came upon a spot

directly above Molly in the water.

"What did you say?" The monkey cupped his hand over his ear.

"What is your name?" Molly asked.

"My name? I'm the monkey of fame, the one with no shame, want to play a game?"

Startled, Molly seemed to be perplexed by the rapid fire rhymes.

"Play a game, I'm not easy to tame, hot as a flame…"

CRACK!!! A pecan hit the monkey on the head and a voice from above shouted, "You're it!" as the monkey started rubbing his head.

Molly grinned and said, "Who's to blame? Now what's your name?"

The monkey looked at Molly, grimaced, rubbed his head, and lowered himself by his tail right in front of Molly's face. "I'm SPENCER THE SPIDER MONKEY."

Molly replied excitedly, "I'm Molly! I'm pretty good at this game, we're the same, me and you… so I want to be a spider monkey too."

Spencer looked Molly up and down and shook his head. "You can't be a spider monkey; you don't have the right kind of tail."

Molly's expression changed. Spencer sensed Molly was upset.

"I know, I know, where you can go!"

"A monkey grasshopper, that's what you are. One lives down the river and not too far." Another pecan whizzed by Spencer's head.

With that Spencer looked over his shoulder, scampered up the tree and out of sight. Molly let out a deep sigh and ducked under the water. She swam down the river.

Molly surfaced near a meadow where she could hear all sorts of sounds. Chirps and whistles and buzzes of every pitch. Suddenly, a beautiful bug hopped on a long piece of grass close to the river.

"Who are you?"

"I am Molly the Manatee. But I want to be a, a, a," she stuttered as she tried to remember what Spencer told her. "A monkey grasshopper!"

"Are you sure? I am **MONICA THE MONKEY GRASSHOPPER,** and you do not look anything like me. Certainly you must be confused?"

"I just do not want to be a manatee anymore, Monica."

"How in the world can you be a monkey grasshopper? You have no legs to hop around. And you cannot be a grasshopper without a hop. I think it's a rule."

Molly sighed deeply. "What in the world can I be, Monica?"

Monica noticed a shadow and looked up to the sky.

"I know you can't be a monkey grasshopper. But perhaps you can be a grasshopper sparrow!"

Monica ducked deep in the grass just as a fleet little bird perched on the twig that Monica had just vacated.

"Where'd she go? Where'd she go?" The sparrow looked around and then

 looked at Molly.

"Who?" replied Molly.

"That tasty little grasshopper."

"I want to be a grasshopper," a confused Molly exclaimed.

"Hmmmm? I don't think you are a grasshopper; you do not look very tasty.

 And grasshoppers are very tasty." The sparrow continued to search for any

 clue as to where the grasshopper might be.

"What is your name?"

"GRAYSON THE GRASSHOPPER SPARROW."

"Grasshopper sparrow? Can I be a grasshopper sparrow?"

"Perhaps... Can you sing?"

"Sing? I have never tried that. How do you sing?"

"How do you sing?"

Grayson began to chirp the most beautiful song.

Molly was delighted to hear such beauty as she closed her eyes and

imagined herself singing in front of her manatee friends.

Molly sang out a low bellow that sounded nothing like Grayson's beautiful singing. Grayson said, "Ugh... Please stop!"

Molly sadly closed her mouth and sank into the river trying to hide. Only her eyes remained above the water.

Grayson motioned for Molly to resurface sensing that he had hurt her feelings. "Look, you don't want to be a grasshopper sparrow anyway. We're too small. You have an athletic build. Why don't you try to be an athletic bird? Like a sparrow hawk?"

Grayson looked over his shoulder and whistled a most delightful sound. He searched the sky. Within a short time a small object appeared. "Spike the Sparrow Hawk!" With those words Grayson flew away into a nearby bush and disappeared.

A small muscular bird quickly approached Molly, flapped his wings, slowed and perched himself on a nearby limb.

"Did you hear that? Did you hear?" the bird asked.

"What? The beautiful song Grayson was singing?" Molly replied.

"Yes. Was it a grasshopper sparrow?"

"Are you SPIKE THE SPARROW HAWK?"

Spike inspected Molly carefully nodding his head yes.

"My name is Molly the Manatee, but Grayson said I'm too athletic to be a grasshopper sparrow. I want to be a sparrow hawk like you."

"No, you can't fly."

With a flap of his wings Spike quickly flew away, looking over his shoulder. He turned and flew back towards Molly. He shouted as he circled once over her head. "You can swim; I bet you could be a hawksbill turtle of the sea." With three quick flaps of his wings, Spike disappeared into the nearby forest.

Molly was sad. She began to swim down the river until she reached the sea.

Molly began to doubt if she would ever even see a turtle in the sea. The sea

was too big. She swam with her head down. Suddenly she hit something hard

with her head.

"Ouch!"

"Ouch yourself!" A deep voice slowly said.

Molly began blinking in disbelief while rubbing her head. "Are you a, a, a?"

she hesitated in confusion.

"I am a sea turtle."

Molly shook her head and grinned. "That is GREAT! I am a manatee. My

name is Molly, and I want to be a sea turtle like you. Do you think it

is possible?"

"Hello, Molly! I am HUGO THE HAWKSBILL TURTLE OF THE SEA. Hmmmm?

Let me see." Hugo looked Molly over. "Well, I do not see why you cannot be

a hawksbill turtle. You swim like a turtle."

Molly had the biggest smile on her face. Finally, she thought she could be something else other than a manatee.

"All you need is your shell." Hugo gently tapped his back making a hard knocking sound.

"Shell? I do not have a shell." Molly tapped her back and that produced a dull thud. "Oh, yes I see, hmmm…You really cannot be a hawksbill turtle without a shell, Molly."

Molly's smile turned to a frown.

Hugo noticed his new friend's sadness and slowly said, "Perhaps you could be a seahorse."

"A seahorse? Where can I find a seahorse?"

"Well, as a matter of fact here comes a whole herd of seahorses now, Molly."

Hugo nodded in the direction behind her.

She looked and saw what appeared to be an approaching cloud. Molly turned to thank Hugo and realized he was swimming away.

Molly was soon surrounded by hundreds of seahorses. They swam so close that they touched her. It tickled her.

Molly managed to stop a very pretty seahorse. "Hello my name is Molly the Manatee."

"Hello Molly, my name is SARA THE SEAHORSE. What is a manatee? Are you a fish?"

"No, I am not a fish. I am a mammal."

Sara looked at Molly and then around at all of the seahorses swimming.

"I wish I could be a manatee then."

Molly looked at Sara and asked, "Why would you want to be a manatee? I think it would be nice to be seahorse."

Each looked at the other for a few moments.

Then Molly said, "You are too small to be a manatee."

"You are too big to be a seahorse," Sara said. "You are big enough to be a horse." Molly looked confused. Sara looked out of the water and told Molly to look on the shore.

There on the shore stood a magnificent animal.

"Go talk to him. He can probably help you with your quest."

Sara turned and disappeared with the rest of the seahorses.

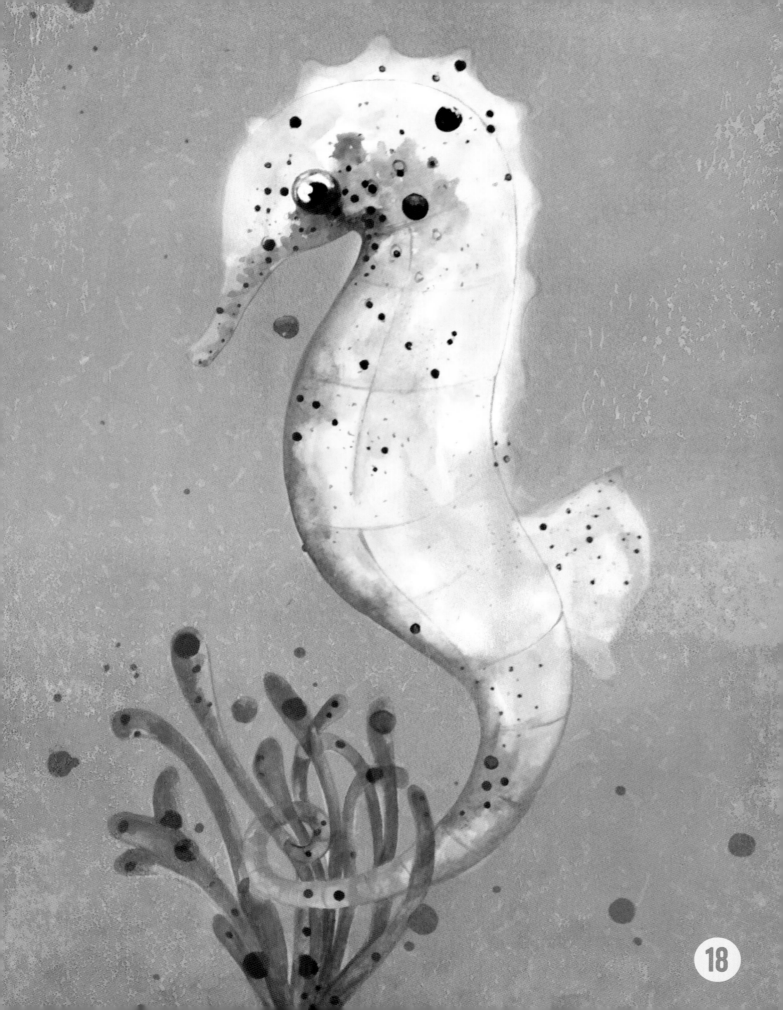

Molly approached the magnificent animal on the shore.

"Hello, my name is Molly. I am a manatee. Are you a horse?"

"Yes! I am HECTOR THE HORSE." He strutted around showing his muscles and swishing his tail.

Molly marveled at the horse and knew that she wanted to be as majestic as Hector.

"Do you think I could be a horse too?" Hector looked at Molly with a puzzled look. "Ummmm? Well, I suppose it is possible." He snapped his tail against his body.

Molly grinned with glee.

Come out of the water and let me see your legs. Horses must have great legs."

Molly's face saddened quickly. "But I don't have legs, just flippers and a tail."

"A horse with no legs—this is not possible!" exclaimed Hector as he looked around quickly and snapped his tail again.

Molly's face grew sadder.

Hector snapped his tail at a horsefly that bit him on his side. "Why don't you leave me alone!"

Molly looked up at Hector and exclaimed, "Rude!"

Hector looked puzzled and then said to Molly, "Not you—her!" as he swished at the horsefly with his tail again and then Hector galloped away.

Suddenly, something flew towards Molly and landed right on Molly's nose.

"You interrupted my meal," exclaimed a funny looking creature with big eyes and clear wings.

"I am sorry. Who or what are you?"

"I am Harriet. **HARRIET THE HORSEFLY**, and you owe me dinner."

Molly looked puzzled.

"Are you a horse? Horses are my favorite meal."

"No, I am Molly the Manatee. I wanted to be a horse, but Hector said I didn't..."

Molly screamed, "Ouch! You just bit me! Why?"

"I was trying to determine if you are a horse. You are not! You taste bad, like a..." Harriet hesitated and looked upward trying to recall a memory.

She saw something flying overhead in the trees.

"A flying squirrel," Harriet exclaimed, and then she flew away.

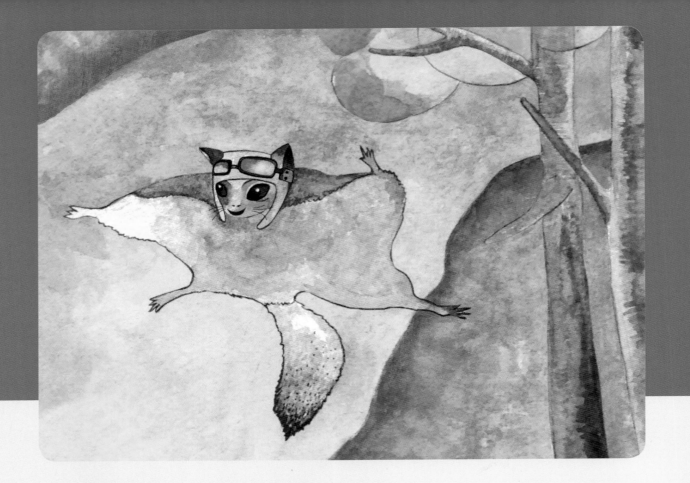

Confused, Molly yelled out in the direction of Harriet. "I taste like a flying squirrel?" She yelled louder. "What is a flying squirrel?"

Out of the branches of the overhanging trees Molly saw something flitting around and making its way to a branch close to the water.

"Did you call for a flying squirrel? My name is **FELIPE THE FLYING SQUIRREL.**"

"Hello Felipe, my name is Molly. I am a manatee."

"You can swim! That looks like so much fun. I wish I could swim."

Molly paused for a moment and thought. "Yes Felipe, I suppose swimming is fun, but I wish I could fly like you."

"Well Molly, maybe swimming is sort of like flying... only under water."

"Hmmm. I never thought of it like that, Felipe. But I want to be out of the water and fly from limb to limb like a flying squirrel."

"I understand that Molly. I really would like to swim in the water. But I cannot and you cannot fly, but you can swim. I know! I have a friend that lives out in the ocean. He is a squirrelfish. Maybe, since you swim like a fish, you can be a squirrelfish."

"A squirrelfish… yes! That sounds like something I could be."

Felipe and Molly talked for a little while longer about the things a flying squirrel and a manatee would discuss. They spoke about swimming and flying and nuts and seagrass and all sorts of interesting things about their lives. Finally, Molly asked for directions to find the squirrelfish and said goodbye to her new friend.

Molly began to swim towards the ocean.

Molly swam to the location in the ocean that Felipe suggested. She searched and searched and saw a most beautiful fish.

"Excuse me, but do you know where I could find the squirrelfish that lives nearby?"

"I am a squirrelfish."

"I am Molly the Manatee. Are you the friend of Felipe the Flying Squirrel?"

"Yes, I am. My name is SQUYRE THE SQUIRRELFISH. How may I help you?"

"Well Squyre, I no longer want to be a manatee. I was wondering if you think I could possibly be a squirrelfish?" Molly asked.

"Molly, you are a manatee, not a squirrelfish. Why do you want to be something other than what you already are?"

"I just want to be something different, something that fits into the rest of the world like a squirrelfish."

"Everything fits into the world in its own way," Squyre said. "I had a very wise being tell me this one day. Perhaps you could go ask him?"

Molly looked exhausted, but managed to ask, "Where can I find him?"

"He is a fisherman. You can find him by listening to the sounds of a motor in the water. Go near the motor sound and he will find you."

Molly swam around and around and listened for very long time. Finally, she heard a little buzzing that sounded as if it were far away. The buzzing became louder and louder. This must be the motor Squyre mentioned. The buzzing became very loud and then suddenly stopped. Molly poked her head out of the water and saw a man standing on what looked like a big log. Molly swam closer.

"Excuse me," she said. "Are you a fisherman?"

The man turned and searched for the voice in the water. When he saw Molly he seemed startled and flipped open the patch covering his eye. He smiled a bright smile that made Molly feel very welcome.

"I am a fisherman; my friends call me **CAPTAIN COLTON**. What is your name manatee?"

"My name is Molly. How do you know I am a manatee?"

"I know all sorts of things about my friends in this world. Manatees are one of my favorite friends."

"Really?"

"Yes. Your kind is legend in these parts. Many years ago men traveled long distances and explored these waters. When they first saw your kind they thought you were mermaids."

"Mermaids? What are those?"

"Well, MERMAIDS were mythical creatures of the sea. They were thought to be the most lovesome and graceful occupants of these waters."

"Really?" Molly asked with a broad smile on her face.

"Yes, and they found them to be extremely gentle creatures. They have always made very nice neighbors to mankind."

Molly's smile was a very broad smile indeed. She said thank you to Captain Colton. Excitedly, she began to swim back to her manatee family and friends.

When Molly finally found her pod she explained her adventure. She described all the creatures she had met and told of the wonderful discoveries she had made. The pod enthusiastically began to plan a surprise for Molly, contacting every creature of whom Molly spoke and inviting them to a great manatee gathering. The following week all the creatures, Molly's family and her friends came together to celebrate Molly's return.

Molly was thrilled with the wonderful variety of friends and family surrounding her! She could now see that each and every one of them had something unique to offer the world around her—as did she, just the way she was—a lovely manatee.

Manatee Facts

Photo June Roberson Gaines

Did you know? Manatees are large, gray aquatic mammals with bodies that taper to a flat, paddle-shaped tail. They have two forelimbs, called flippers, with three to four nails on each flipper. Their head and face are wrinkled with whiskers on the snout. The manatee's closest relatives are the elephant and the hyrax (a small, gopher-sized mammal). Manatees are believed to have evolved from a wading, plant-eating animal. The West Indian Manatee is related to the West African Manatee, the Amazonian Manatee, the dugong, and Steller's sea cow, which was hunted to extinction in 1768. The average adult manatee is about 10 feet long and weighs between 800 and 1,200 pounds.

HABITAT AND RANGE: Manatees can be found in shallow, slow-moving rivers, estuaries, saltwater bays, canals, and coastal areas—particularly where seagrass beds or freshwater vegetation flourish. Manatees are a migratory species. Within the United States, they are concentrated in Florida in the winter. In summer months, they can be found as far west as Texas and as far north as Massachusetts, but summer sightings in Alabama, Georgia, and South Carolina are more common.

CREDIT: Save the Manatee Club. See more at: http://www.savethemanatee.org

A portion of the proceeds from this book is given to savethemanatee.org

Let's play How Many?

Now that you have read "Molly the Manatee" go back
and count how many characters

A How many monkeys can you find within the story?

B How many birds?

C How many manatees?

D How many fish (not including seahorses)?

E How many seahorses?

F How many trees?

G Which is your favorite?

Chic Cariaga Chic has been writing since his high school days in Charlotte, North Carolina. Part poet, part Southern Renaissance story-teller, and part world wandering writer; Chic's path has led him to the place he was destined to be… writing is his home. Spinning bedtime tales to his sons Grayson and Colton has led him to scribe his first children's book. And so the journey continues, many trails to trace and stories to write.

Liza Donovan Liza is a Graphic Designer and artist living in Charlotte. She has always been a passionate art lover and project enthusiast. She turns to art for expression and is inspired by the culture and fashion of the 60s, American post-punk posters, Eastern European poster art, and cats every-where. Drawn to the nonsensical and playful, Liza insists on work being fun.

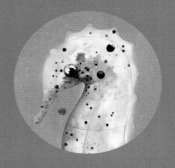

Sara the Seahorse

Seahorses live in shallow tropical waters. They don't have scales even though they look like they do and swim upright which is very different from other aquatic life. They don't swim very well and rely on the dorsal fin to help them move. The two eyes of a seahorse are able to move independently of each other.

Hector the Horse

Domestic horses have a lifespan of around 25 years, can sleep both lying down and standing up, and can run shortly after birth. Their eyes are bigger than any other mammal on land and placement on the side of its head makes them capable of seeing nearly 360 degrees at one time. The fastest recorded sprinting speed of a horse was 55 mph.

Harriet the Horsefly

The horsefly egg is laid on plants in or near water. Once they hatch, horsefly larvae will spend one to two years growing in moist soil or water. As an adult, they only live for a few days. If a horsefly lands on you and bites, it is a female fly.

Felipe the Flying Squirrel

Flying squirrels can't fly like birds but they can glide between trees. Flying squirrels have been known to glide for distances of up to 295 feet. All squirrels are born blind.